I Like to Visit/Me gusta visitar

The Museum/
El museo

Jacqueline Laks Gorman

Reading consultant/Consultora de lectura:
Susan Nations, M. Ed.,
author, literacy coach, consultant/
autora, tutora de alfabetización, consultora

Please visit our web site at: www.earlyliteracy.cc
For a free color catalog describing Weekly Reader® Early Learning Library's list
of high-quality books, call 1-877-445-5824 (USA) or 1-800-387-3178 (Canada).
Weekly Reader® Early Learning Library's fax: (414) 336-0164.

Library of Congress Cataloging-in-Publication Data available upon request from publisher.
Fax (414) 336-0157 for the attention of the Publishing Records Department.

ISBN 0-8368-4597-8 (lib. bdg.)
ISBN 0-8368-4604-4 (softcover)

This edition first published in 2005 by
Weekly Reader® Early Learning Library
330 West Olive Street, Suite 100
Milwaukee, WI 53212 USA

Copyright © 2005 by Weekly Reader® Early Learning Library

Art direction: Tammy West
Editor: JoAnn Early Macken
Cover design and page layout: Kami Koenig
Picture research: Diane Laska-Swanke
Translator: Tatiana Acosta and Guillermo Gutiérrez

Picture credits: Cover, pp. 5, 7, 9, 11, 13, 15, 17, 19, 21 Gregg Andersen

Printed in the United States of America

1 2 3 4 5 6 7 8 9 09 08 07 06 05

Note to Educators and Parents

Reading is such an exciting adventure for young children! They are beginning to integrate their oral language skills with written language. To encourage children along the path to early literacy, books must be colorful, engaging, and interesting; they should invite the young reader to explore both the print and the pictures.

I Like to Visit is a new series designed to help children read about familiar and exciting places. Each book explores a different place that kids like to visit and describes what a visitor can see and do there.

Each book is specially designed to support the young reader in the reading process. The familiar topics are appealing to young children and invite them to read — and re-read — again and again. The full-color photographs and enhanced text further support the student during the reading process.

In addition to serving as wonderful picture books in schools, libraries, homes, and other places where children learn to love reading, these books are specifically intended to be read within an instructional guided reading group. This small group setting allows beginning readers to work with a fluent adult model as they make meaning from the text. After children develop fluency with the text and content, the book can be read independently. Children and adults alike will find these books supportive, engaging, and fun!

— **Susan Nations, M.Ed., author/literacy coach/reading consultant**

Nota para los educadores y los padres

¡Leer es una aventura tan emocionante para los niños pequeños! A esta edad están comenzando a integrar su manejo del lenguaje oral con el lenguaje escrito. Para animar a los niños en el camino de la lectura incipiente, los libros deben ser coloridos, estimulantes e interesantes; deben invitar a los jóvenes lectores a explorar la letra impresa y las ilustraciones.

Me gusta visitar es una nueva colección diseñada para que los niños lean textos sobre lugares familiares y emocionantes. Cada libro explora un lugar diferente que a los niños les gustaría visitar, y describe lo que se puede ver y hacer en cada sitio.

Cada libro está especialmente diseñado para ayudar a los jóvenes lectores en el proceso de lectura. Los temas familiares llaman la atención de los niños y los invitan a leer —y releer— una y otra vez. Las fotografías a todo color y el tamaño de la letra ayudan aún más al estudiante en el proceso de lectura.

Además de servir como maravillosos libros ilustrados en escuelas, bibliotecas, hogares y otros lugares donde los niños aprenden a amar la lectura, estos libros han sido especialmente concebidos para ser leídos en un grupo de lectura guiada. Este contexto permite que los lectores incipientes trabajen con un adulto que domina la lectura mientras van determinando el significado del texto. Una vez que los niños dominan el texto y el contenido, el libro puede ser leído de manera independiente. ¡Estos libros les resultarán útiles, estimulantes y divertidos a niños y a adultos por igual!

— **Susan Nations, M.Ed., autora/tutora de alfabetización/consultora de desarrollo de la lectura**

I like to visit the children's museum.
I can learn about science there.
I can learn about the stars. A group
of stars is called a **constellation**.

■ ■ ■ ■ ■ ■ ■

Me gusta visitar el museo de los
niños. Allí puedo aprender ciencias.
Puedo aprender cosas sobre las
estrellas. Un grupo de estrellas
forman una **constelación**.

I can learn about how things work.
I can learn about sound. Music is a
kind of sound.

— — — — — — —

En el museo puedo aprender
cómo funcionan las cosas.
Puedo conocer los sonidos.
La música es un tipo de sonido.

I can learn about my body at the museum. I can play with a model. I can fit the parts inside.

■ ■ ■ ■ ■ ■ ■

En el museo puedo aprender cosas sobre mi cuerpo. Puedo jugar con un modelo. Puedo poner las partes en su sitio.

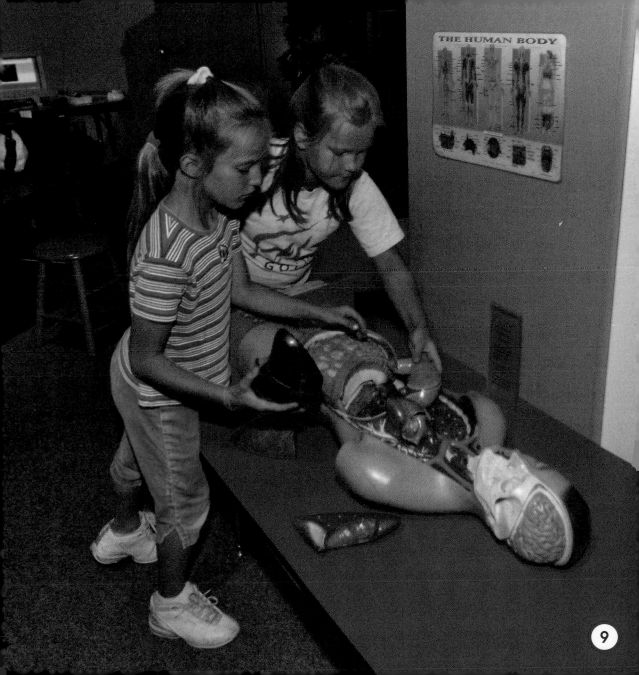

THE HUMAN BODY

I can learn about animals. I can learn where they live. Most lions live in Africa.

- - - - - - -

También puedo aprender cosas sobre los animales. Puedo aprender dónde viven. La mayoría de los leones viven en África.

Bears in Africa?

Not today. But two million years ago, a huge, long-legged bear—*Agriotherium*—hunted on the savanna. This bear preyed on animals the size of a buffalo or larger.

I can find fossils at the museum.

The fossils are from long ago.

They are from plants and animals.

- - - - - - -

En el museo puedo ver fósiles.

Los fósiles son muy antiguos. Se
formaron con plantas y animales.

I can learn about space at the museum. I can learn about a ship that went into space.

En el museo puedo aprender cosas sobre el espacio. Puedo conocer una nave que voló al espacio.

DOCKING THE REAL
SPACE SHUTTLE

I can learn about rocks at the museum. I can see many kinds of rocks. I can even see rocks that came from space!

En el museo puedo aprender cosas sobre las rocas. Puedo ver muchos tipos de rocas. ¡Hasta puedo ver rocas que vinieron del espacio!

WHAT IS IT?
hint: Find the picture of rough, broken lava.

WHAT IS IT?
hint: Find the picture of a lava "fountain" (like fireworks).

I can see dinosaurs at the museum.
I can see their footprints. I can see
their bones, too.

‑ ‑ ‑ ‑ ‑ ‑ ‑

En el museo puedo ver dinosaurios.
Puedo ver sus huellas. También
puedo ver sus huesos.

Some dinosaurs were big and scary. Would you like to see a dinosaur?

——————————

Algunos dinosaurios eran muy grandes y daban mucho miedo. ¿Te gustaría ver un dinosaurio?

Glossary

constellation — a group of stars that seems to form a picture

dinosaurs — reptiles that lived on Earth millions of years ago

fossils — remains or tracks of animals or plants that lived long ago

museum — a place where people can see interesting collections of things about science, art, or history

science — the study of nature and the world

Glosario

ciencias — estudio de la naturaleza y el mundo

constelación — grupo de estrellas que parece que formaran un dibujo

dinosaurios — reptiles que vivieron en la Tierra hace millones de años

fósiles — restos o huellas de animales o plantas que existieron hace mucho tiempo

museo — lugar donde las personas pueden ver colecciones interesantes de cosas relacionadas con las ciencias, el arte o la historia

For More Information/Más información

Books

Class Trip. Mercer Mayer (McGraw-Hill)
The Natural Science Museum. Field Trip! (series).
  Angela Leeper (Heinemann)

Libros

*Mi visita a los dinosaurios/My Visit to the
  Dinosaurs.* Aliki (Editorial Juventud)
Franklin en el museo/Franklin's Class Trip.
  Paulette Bourgeois (Sagebrush)

Web Sites

Children's Discovery Museum of San Jose
www.cdm.org/
Explore, play games, and learn

Páginas Web

Quest
www.nhm.ac.uk/education/quest2/espanol/
Museo de Historia Natural de Londres

Index

índice

About the Author

Jacqueline Laks Gorman is a writer and editor. She grew up in New York City and began her career working on encyclopedias and other reference books. Since then, she has worked on many different kinds of books and written several children's books. She lives with her husband, David, and children, Colin and Caitlin, in DeKalb, Illinois. They all like to visit many kinds of places.

Información sobre la autora

Jacqueline Laks Gorman trabaja como escritora y editora. Jacqueline creció en la ciudad de Nueva York y comenzó su carrera trabajando en enciclopedias y otros libros de referencia. Desde entonces, ha trabajado en distintos tipos de libros y ha escrito varios libros para niños. Jacqueline vive con su esposo, David, y sus hijos, Colin y Caitlin, en DeKalb, Illinois. A toda la familia le gusta visitar distintos lugares.